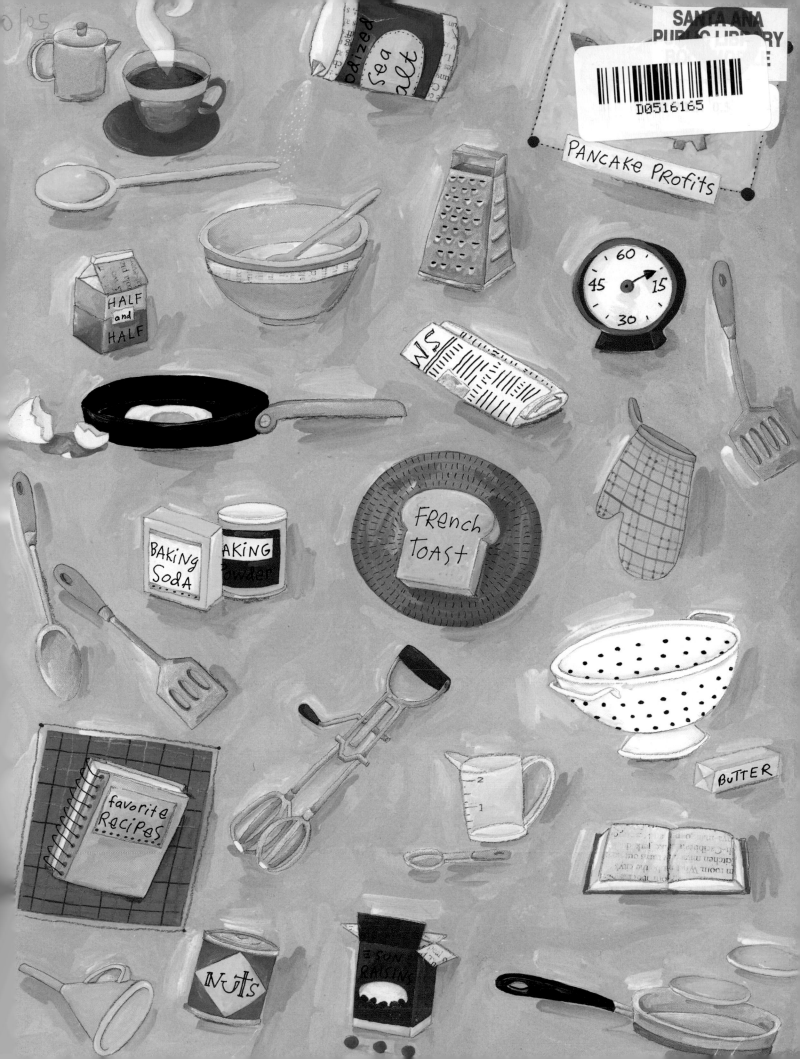

For my mother

Henry Holt and Company, LLC, *Publishers since 1866*
115 West 18th Street, New York, New York 10011
www.henryholt.com

Henry Holt is a registered trademark of Henry Holt and Company, LLC
Copyright © 2005 by Nancy Wolff. All rights reserved.
Distributed in Canada by H. B. Fenn and Company Ltd.

Library of Congress Cataloging-in-Publication Data
Wolff, Nancy. Tallulah in the kitchen / by Nancy Wolff.—1st ed.
p.   cm.
Summary: Tallulah the cat and her friends experiment with a new recipe for pancakes.
ISBN-13: 978-0-8050-7463-5
ISBN-10: 0-8050-7463-5
[1. Cookery—Fiction. 2. Pancakes, waffles, etc.—Fiction. 3. Cats—Fiction.] I. Title.
PZ7.W821255Tal 2005   [E]—dc22   2004009201
First Edition—2005 / Designed by Nancy Wolff
Printed in the United States of America on acid-free paper. ∞

The artist used gouache on Canson paper
to create the illustrations for this book.

10 9 8 7 6 5 4 3 2 1

TALLulah

in the kitchen

by NANCY WOLFF

Henry Holt and Company
New York

THiS CAT reALLY COOKS!

This is Tallulah.
She loves to cook.

Sometimes Tallulah gets help from her friends Freddie and Roxy and her dog, Flapjack. They have been pals since their sandbox days, when Tallulah instructed them in the fine art of mud-pie making. Today they are going to be Tallulah's product testers.

Tallulah's specialty is pancakes, and she's always experimenting with new recipe varieties.

Just last week she invented the chocolate chip flip with mini marshmallows and sliced bananas. It was Freddie's favorite. The worst pancake Tallulah ever made was filled with coconut and jelly beans.

RULES

1. Don't even think about cooking in the kitchen without an adult at your side (If you count in cat years, Tallulah is much older than she looks.)

2. Oven mitts are a must when handling hot pots and pans.

3. Always dress properly. Colorful clothes will hide most dribbles and spots. Plaids are best. Stripes and polka dots work too.

4. Put on a hat — it will make you look and feel professional.

Freddie, that tie is a potential hazard. Roxy, your button looks a little loose. Flapjack, lose the sweater.

Before the cooking session can begin, Tallulah must . . .

. . . decide on a recipe and check to see
what ingredients she has at home . . .

. . . make
a list of the
things she
needs . . .

. . . and take a trip
to the grocery store.

The baking aisle is Tallulah's favorite place to shop. She does her best daydreaming here. Once she has her supplies, Tallulah heads home to start cooking.

recipe

1 ¼ cups FLOUR

2 ½ teaspoons baking Powder

½ teaspoon Salt

1 TABLESPOON Sugar

1 egg well beaten

1 cup MILK

3 tablespoons oil CANOLA oil

2 cups Blueberries

Makes about 12 4-inch Pancakes

Today sweet butter and oil as needed to coat skillet

Amazing Blueberryalicious Pancakes

First Tallulah measures the flour and pours it into a large bowl. This can get a little messy.

Cough Cough!

FLOUR

What does a dog have to do to get some food around here?

1 Freddie, with help from Tallulah, carefully measures the baking powder and salt.

2 Oh, no! I feel a sneeze coming on.

3

4 Freddie then adds these ingredients to the flour.

5

Next Roxy sprinkles in the proper amount of sugar.

6

AH AH AH AH

Talk about a secret ingredient.

I'm almost afraid to look!

7

That was close.

Whew!

8

TALLULAH sets the bowl aside for later.

Now for the egg. Cracking an egg into a bowl is tricky and takes some practice. Thankfully, there are a dozen eggs in a carton. (HINT: If an eggshell finds its way into the batter, do your best to fish it out, then add something crunchy to the mix, like nuts, just in case.) Freddie likes to beat the egg. On good days, most of it stays in the bowl.

In the same bowl with the egg, Tallulah adds the milk and then the oil.

Tallulah's Glossary of unscientific Cooking Terms

dab - 2 tsp.
dollop - 1 tbsp.
Pinch - $\frac{1}{8}$ tsp.
Smidgen - 1 tsp.
Splash - 1 oz.

Feed them a pancake a day and your loved ones won't stray.

MILK

Note to beginners: Follow the recipe. Creativity for those new to the kitchen can have disastrous results.

Tallulah lets Freddie slowly pour the milk, egg, and oil mixture into the bowl with the flour and sugar. She then stirs everything together.

Steady, Freddie.

Some things to keep in mind

A. Lumps are okay.
B. Too much stirring will result in thick, heavy Pancakes that sit in your tummy for an entire day.
C. Four hands are better than two hands.
D. Never sneeze directly into the batter.

Before the blueberries make it into the batter, they must be examined thoroughly. As official berry cleaner, Roxy is responsible for weeding out any stems, pebbles, worms, and bugs. Roxy considers bugs a good source of protein as well as a nice extra crunch, but Tallulah disagrees, so Roxy pockets all bugs for later snacking. Worms she can happily live without. Once this task is done, Roxy adds the berries to the batter.

The GREAT Chefs Tell ALL

Now that everything is mixed together in one bowl,
Tallulah heads for the stove to prepare her frying pan.

No matter how many batches I've made in my lives, I still get goose bumps before each flip.

Tallulah favors a mixture of butter and oil in her skillet—a splash of oil for every dab of butter. Today she is making medium-size pancakes and can fit four in the pan at once.

Spatula in hand, Tallulah peers into the frying pan for what seems like a long time. Freddie, Roxy, and Flapjack watch Tallulah watching the pancakes. Is she waiting for a signal? Then the first pancake bubbles and Tallulah springs into action. What a beautiful flip! And another, again, and once more! She's in perfect form.

Flip to finish, a pancake usually takes about thirty seconds to cook. Tallulah remains focused on her cooking tasks while Freddie and Roxy are on timing duty. After the first twenty seconds go by, Roxy and Freddie do the countdown together.

10 9 8 7 6 5 4 3 2 1

They are READY!

I'm starved!

Woof

The first batch looks delicious. The next few look delicious too. Before long, Tallulah has a great big stack of mouth-watering pancakes. *Mmmmm.* Tallulah's pancakes are not always round, but that's okay, they still taste good.

CAUTION: Try not to reAd this book on an empty stomach.

Cleanup is never as much fun as cooking.
Here are some helpful tips.

Helpful Tips

1. Remember to wipe all spills quickly so no one slips or falls.

2. Gooey batter gets hard and crusty in minutes.

3. Everyone working together makes the job go faster.

4. There are times when a bath is necessary.

Occasionally, Tallulah likes to dazzle her friends with her international pancake knowledge.

So far she's sampled crêpes, flat French pancakes that are rolled and sometimes set on fire—a meal and a show!

She has also tried tortillas, Mexican pancakes made of cornmeal.

And soon Tallulah plans to taste Russian blinis. Blinis are often served with caviar and sour cream.

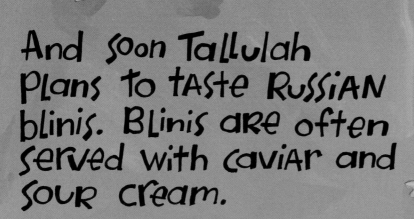

Making your own pancakes is great fun and talking about them is nice too. But eating them is the best of all. Tallulah and her buddies gather at the kitchen table and choose their toppings. Roxy goes for lots of syrup. Freddie prefers powdered sugar. Tallulah likes the syrup-on-the-side method of cutting and dunking. Flapjack, for dietary reasons, has his plain.

After sampling and analyzing the pancakes and complimenting each other on their delicate flavor, the cooks take the leftovers outside. It's nice to share what you make with others. (Hint: It's also nice to make a profit.)

Tallulah hopes to be a famous chef someday, with her own restaurant and maybe even a cooking show on television. For now, she is happy sharing her pancakes with Freddie, Roxy, and Flapjack, and turning a little profit when she can.